For Guillaume
M·E·
For Stewart
G·R·

Reprinted 1996

First published in 1995 by Magi Publications
55 Crowland Avenue, Hayes, Middx UB3 4JP

This edition published in 1995

Text © 1995 by Mark Ezra
Illustrations © 1995 by Gavin Rowe

Typeset in Galliard Roman

Printed and bound in Belgium by
Proost N.V., Turnhout

ISBN 1 85430 128 4

MARK EZRA

The Prickly Hedgehog

pictures by GAVIN ROWE

Magi Publications, London

It was Little Hedgehog's first day out.
His mother was leading a food hunt,
and he hurried along behind his four prickly
brothers and sisters as fast as his short legs
could carry him. But it was no good.
In no time at all he was left way behind.

A big butterfly landed on Little Hedgehog's
snout. He tried to brush it off, but it fluttered
away over his head and he overbalanced.
By the time he had picked himself up,
his family had completely disappeared.

"They can't have gone far," thought
Little Hedgehog, pulling off all the dry
leaves that were stuck to his coat.
"That feels better," he said, as he set off to
look for them.

Oh good, there they were in the clearing ahead!
Little Hedgehog grunted with joy.
He scuttled forward, but all he
found was . . .

. . . a circle of hedgehog mushrooms
with little spines poking out from
under their caps.
"Mm, these look good to eat," he said,
and he stuck four of them on his back.
"But where *are* my family?" he wondered
very sadly.

Ah, there they were, at the foot of that hedge! Little Hedgehog's eyes lit up and his heart beat faster. But when he got there, all he found was a broken teasel twig with some teasels on it.

"Wrong again!" said Little Hedgehog.
He ran on, and bumped into a big tree.
"How tall it is!" he said, looking upwards.
"But what's that up there?"

High up on a branch Little
Hedgehog thought he saw his
family. It seemed an awfully long
way to climb, but some ivy grew up
the tree and it gave him
a foothold.

Twig by twig and branch by branch
he climbed up through the leaves.
He teetered along a thin bough
towards the spiny little group.
He had never been so scared in
his life, but he knew he must be
brave and not look down.

When he reached them,
Little Hedgehog saw that
his climb was in vain.
"Stupid me!" he exclaimed,
for they were only a bunch
of spiny chestnuts.

He reached out and stuck four on
his back. It wasn't easy, and when he
turned round he lost his balance
and fell . . .

. . . and as he fell down and down, he curled into a tight ball and bounced onto a soft bed of leaves. "Bother!" said Little Hedgehog, wriggling round to pull the leaves from his spiny back.

Suddenly Little Hedgehog heard a loud noise, and an enormous creature bounded up to him. He didn't know it was a friendly dog. He was absolutely terrified. Once again, he curled right up into a tight ball to protect himself.

Moments passed.
Had the creature gone?
Little Hedgehog uncurled,
and to his horror he saw the
dog's big head bending
down towards him . . .

The dog picked him up in his powerful jaws,
and trotted along the path with him.
Then, just as suddenly, he dropped him.
The frightened little hedgehog landed on
a soft mossy bank.

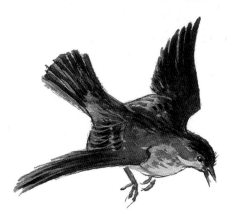

Little Hedgehog stayed curled
up for a long time.
He was still very frightened.
Then suddenly he heard some
familiar snorting sounds.
He opened his eyes . . .

. . . and there was his mother
and his brothers and sisters!
"Where have you been?"
asked his mother.

Little Hedgehog uncurled
himself.
"Oh, just hunting for food,"
he said. "See what I've brought
back for you!"

His mother looked at the feast of food
on Little Hedgehog's back.
"Mushrooms and chestnuts!" cried all his
brothers and sisters. They all tucked
in till their tummies were quite full.
Then they fell asleep under their
favourite hedge.

Little Hedgehog's mother licked his face
clean, and found him some ripe berries.
The prickly little hedgehog never told his
mother all about his adventures, but I think
she must have guessed.
Don't you?